Ebenezer
Opens a
Savings Account

By Tiffany Alexander
Illustrated by Dontay Barnes

Ebenezer Opens a Savings Account

ISBN 978-0-9820039-3-0

For further information visit:
www.childrensband.com
Email: info@childrensband.com

Ebenezer spent Saturday morning doing his chores.

1

He washed the breakfast dishes.

He raked the leaves in his backyard.

3

He put his dirty clothes in the hamper and cleaned his bedroom.

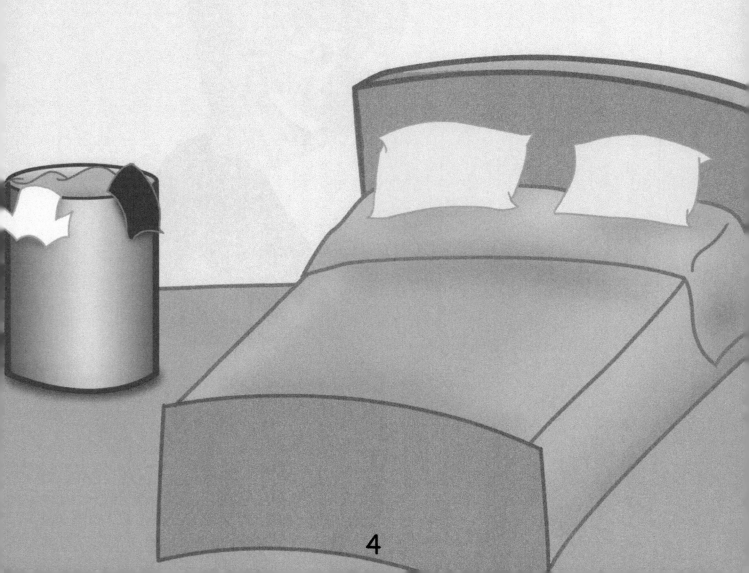

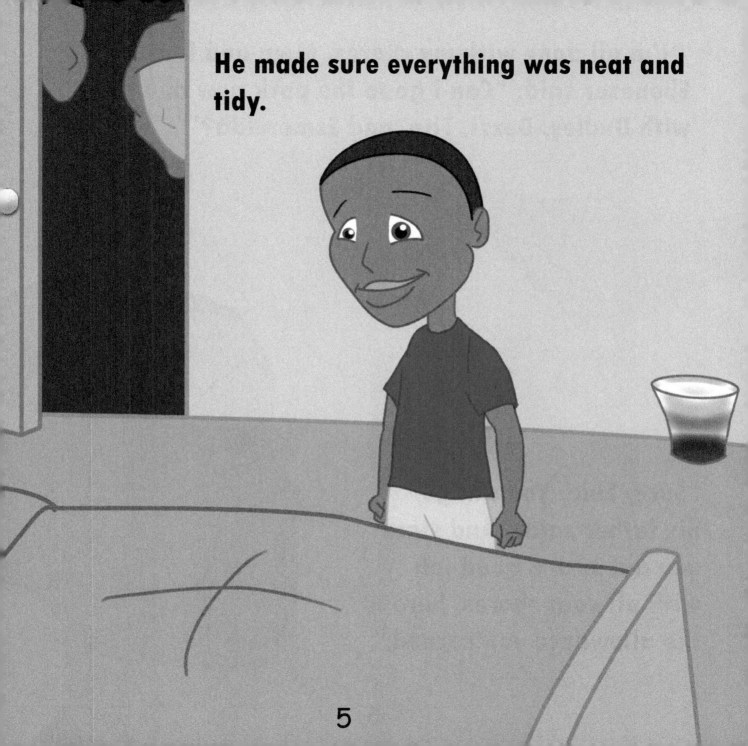

He made sure everything was neat and tidy.

"I'm all done with my chores, Mom and Dad,"
Ebenezer said. "Can I go to the park now and play
with Dudley, Dezzi, Tito, and Esmerelda?"

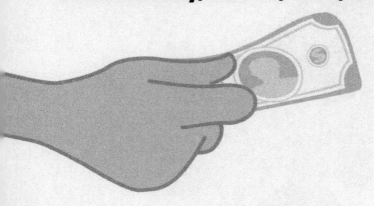

"Sure, Ebie. You can go,"
his father said. "And since
you did such a good job
with all your chores, here is
the allowance you earned."

What are you going to do with all your money?" his mother asked.

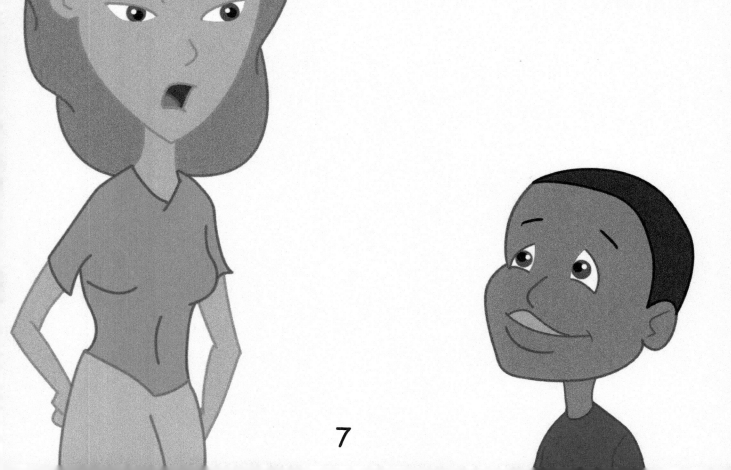

"I'll spend some of it on snacks and books," Ebie said. "I'll put the rest of it in my piggy bank. When I have enough money, I'm going to buy a new computer."

"Ebie, we are so proud of you for saving your money," his mother said.

9

"Yes we are, son," his father said. "I think I should take you to the bank so you can open your first savings account."

"I don't understand," Ebie said. "What's a savings account?"

ngs account is a safe place to put your money," rather explained. "Your mother and I both have savings accounts at the bank."

12

"Every week, we put money in our savings accounts," his mother said. "When we need to buy something important, we go to the bank and get the money out."

13

"Something important like a new computer? Or a video game? Or a music player?" Ebie was very excited.

14

"That's right," his parents said.

Ebie couldn't wait to open his very own savings account.

16

"When can we go to the bank?"
He asked.

"I'll take you to the bank when
you get home from the park," his
father said.

17

Ebie walked to the park to meet his friends. He thought of all the things he could buy if he saved his money.

"Guess what, everyone," he said. "My dad is going to take me to the bank to open my first savings account."

"What's a savings account?" Dezzi asked.

"It's a safe place to keep my money," Ebie explained. "I will keep putting money in the bank until I save enough to buy something important. I'm going to save my money and buy a computer."

"If I put my money in the bank, I can save enough to buy a computer, too," Esmerelda said. "Maybe I will buy a telescope so I can look at the stars at night."

I'm going to save enough money to buy a new bicycle," Tito said. "I want new Rollerblades and running shoes, too."

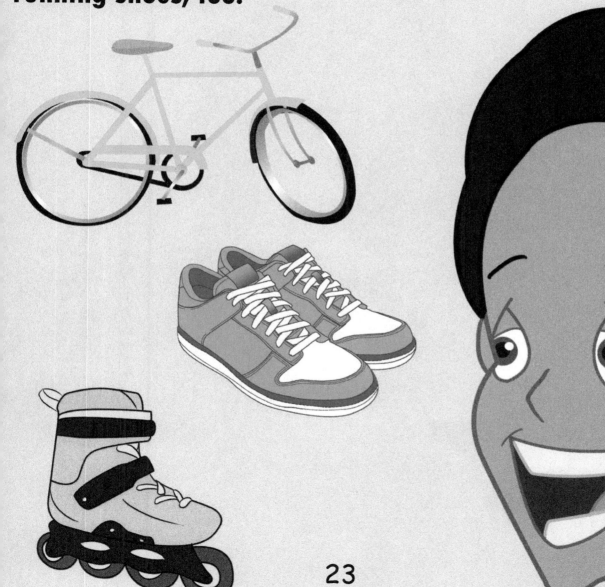

23

"I'm going to save my money and buy a violin, and new clothes for ballet class," Dezzi said.

"If I save my money, I can buy a nice gift for my dad," Dudley signed. "I can get a new doghouse for my dog Ginger, too."

25

"I have an idea," Tito said. "Let's ask our parents if we can have savings accounts, too."

Tito, Dezzi, Esmerelda, and Dudley were very happy that their friend Ebie taught them about savings accounts.

That afternoon Ebie's mother and father took him to the bank.

28

"Hello. My name is Ebenezer, and I'm here to open my first savings account," Ebie told the bank teller.

His mom and dad took him to the bank every week so he could put more money into his savings account.

When Ebie saved enough money, his father took him to the computer store. He picked out the computer he wanted and paid for it with money from his savings account.

"Congratulations, son," his father said. "I'm proud of you."

31

Ebie was proud of himself, too. "Thanks for teaching me how to save money, Dad."

32

Children's Band books were created
to inspire and educate all kids.

EBENEZER is a young entrepreneur.
ESMERELDA is a future scientist.
DEZZI loves arts and culture.
TITO encourages a healthy diet and exercise.
DUDLEY is deaf, but he knows that even
though he is different, God still has a plan for his
life.

To meet the members
of Children's Band visit
www.childrensband.com

CPSIA information can be obtained at www.ICGtesting.com
Printed in the USA
LVOW02s1546040615

441213LV00001B/1/P